W9-AZT-497

Drakestail

adapted from a French folktale by
Jan Wahl

illustrated by
Byron Barton

Greenwillow Books
A Division of William Morrow & Company, Inc., New York

Library of Congress Cataloging in Publication Data
Wahl, Jan.   Drakestail.   (Greenwillow read-alone series)
Summary: The adventures of a drake who becomes a king
with the help of a fox, ladder, river, and waspnest.
[1. Folklore—France]   I. Barton, Byron.   II. Title
PZ8.1.W126Dr   398.2'452'0944   [E]   77-24331
ISBN 0-688-80126-9   ISBN 0-688-84126-0 lib. bdg.

FOR FRANCES WOOD

Drakestail was little.

He also had brains.

He saved his money.

The King, who spent
all his money,
came to Drakestail
to borrow some.

But years went by
and the King had not
paid back a penny.

So one fine morning,

Drakestail, fresh and shiny,

decided to go and see the King.

He walked down the road, singing,

   "Quack, quack, quack!

   When will I get

   My money back?"

He met friend Fox.

"Where are you off to?"

"I am off to the King
to fetch my money,"
said Drakestail.

"Oh, take me with you!"

You can't have too many friends,
thought Drakestail.

"I will," he said.

"But walking on all fours,

you'll soon be tired.

Make yourself tiny,

climb into my throat,

jump into my gizzard,

and I will carry you."

"Terrific!" said Fox.

He took bag and baggage
and down he jumped
like a letter in a mailbox.

Fresh and shiny,

Drakestail was off again,

singing,

    "Quack, quack, quack!

    When will I get

    My money back?"

He had not gone far when
he met his girl friend, Lady Ladder.
She was leaning against a wall.
"Good morning, duckling," she said.
"Where are you off to?"

"I am off to the King

to fetch my money."

"Oh take me with you!"

You can't have too many friends,

thought Drakestail.

"I will," he said.

"But with your wooden legs,

you'll soon be tired.

Make yourself tiny,

climb into my throat,

jump in my gizzard,

and I will carry you."

"Terrific!" said Lady Ladder.

She took bag and baggage

and down she jumped,

easy as anything.

"Quack, quack, quack!
When will I get
My money back?"
said Drakestail
and strutted away.

In a little bit he met

his sweetheart, Madam River.

She was wandering along

in the sunshine.

"Good morning, angel," she said.

"Where are you off to?"

Drakestail said,

"I'm off to the King

to fetch my money."

"Oh, take me with you!"

You can't have too many friends,

thought Drakestail.

"I will," he said.

"But moving along without feet,

you'll soon be tired.

Make yourself tiny,

climb into my throat,

jump in my gizzard,

and I will carry you."

"Terrific!" said Madam River.
She took bag and baggage
and down she jumped—
glub, glub, glub!

Drakestail waddled on his way,
singing,

   "Quack, quack, quack!

   When will I get

   My money back?"

On top of a hill
he met old General Waspnest.
The General was marching
with his army of wasps.
"Good morning, sir.
Where are you off to?"
asked the General.

"I'm off to the King

to fetch my money."

"Oh, take me with you!"

You can't have too many friends,

thought Drakestail.

"I will," he said.

"But with an army to drag along,

you'll soon be tired.

Make yourself tiny,

climb into my throat,

jump in my gizzard,

and I will carry you."

"Terrific!" said General Waspnest.

With a big buzz he slipped in, too.

It was crowded inside,

but they all managed.

Left, right! Left, right!

Drakestail marched gaily

into town, singing loudly,

   "Quack, quack, quack!

   When will I get

   My money back?"

He rapped at the King's

tall oak door.

"The King is eating,"

the porter said. "Wait here."

He went upstairs
to tell the King
a duck had come.

"Good!" the King laughed.
"Put him in with the chickens
and turkeys."

The porter came downstairs.

"This way, duck," he said.

"Good!" Drakestail thought

he was going to the King.

But the porter led him
to the chicken yard.
When they arrived,
he pushed Drakestail into the coop.

"What is THIS?"

Huge birds attacked him.

They bit and snapped.

Drakestail cried,

"Foxie, step quick!

Sharp beaks do prick!"

When friend Fox heard,
he stepped out and made
short work of the birds.

And Drakestail sang,

"Quack, quack, quack!
When will I get
My money back?"

The chicken girl hurried
to tell the King.
"Toss him into the well!"
shouted the King.

Drakestail was thrown

into the well.

Drakestail cried,

"Lady Ladder! Oh be swift!
Your friend Drakestail
Needs a lift."

Lady Ladder raised her arms
and Drakestail climbed
up her back out of the well.

And Drakestail sang,

    "Quack quack, quack!

    WHEN will I get

    My money back?"

The King was still at table.

"Toss that duck
into the furnace!"
he shouted.

So Drakestail was thrown
into the furnace.

Drakestail cried,

"Madam River!

The flames grow higher!

Run to me

and quench this fire!"

Madam River rushed out.
She drowned the hot coals
and spilled over the floor
in a flood.

Drakestail swam down the hall
and again sang,

"Quack, quack, quack!
WHEN will I get

my money back?"

The King picked up
his knife and fork.
"Where is he? Let me at him!"

Two footmen led Drakestail in.

"Hurray," said Drakestail.

"The King wishes to see me at last!"

But the King, hot as fire,

red as turkey,

held a big sword in his hand.

Drakestail cried,

"Waspnest!

Save me from the King!

Send your army out to

Sting! Sting! Sting!"

Old General Waspnest
sent out his army.
Bsss! Bsss! The army of wasps
stung the King and footmen.

They leaped out the window
and were killed.

Drakestail was alone.

He remembered why he had come,
and he hunted all over
for his dear money.
Drakestail could not find a penny.
Every drawer was empty.

Drakestail looked in all the rooms.

At last he came to

the Throne Room. "What a day!"

He sank down on the soft throne.

The people saw their King
lying outside the palace.
"The King is dead!" they cried.

They saw Drakestail

sitting on the throne.

"Long live the King!" they shouted.

"Put the crown on his head!"

They placed the sparkling crown

on Drakestail's head.

"Maybe this King will not

spend so much money!"

they whispered among themselves.

Drakestail was King!

And he was hungry.

"Thank you, ladies and gentlemen,"

King Drakestail said.

"Let's go to supper."